I DON'T WANT TO BE A FROG

For Chris, Clio, and Isla—who make everything fun.
—D.P.

For Eli, because you're you.
—M.B.

ISBN 978-1-338-26682-5

Text copyright © 2015 by Dev Petty. Cover art and interior illustrations © 2015 by Mike Boldt.
All rights reserved. Published by Scholastic Inc., 557 Broadway, New York, NY 10012,
by arrangement with Random House Children's Books, a division of Penguin Random House LLC.
SCHOLASTIC and associated logos are trademarks and/or registered trademarks of Scholastic Inc.

12 11 10 9 8 7 6 5 4 3 2 1   18 19 20 21 22 23

Printed in the U.S.A.   08

This edition first printing, January 2018

I DON'T WANT TO BE A FROG

written by Dev Petty

illustrated by Mike Boldt

SCHOLASTIC INC.

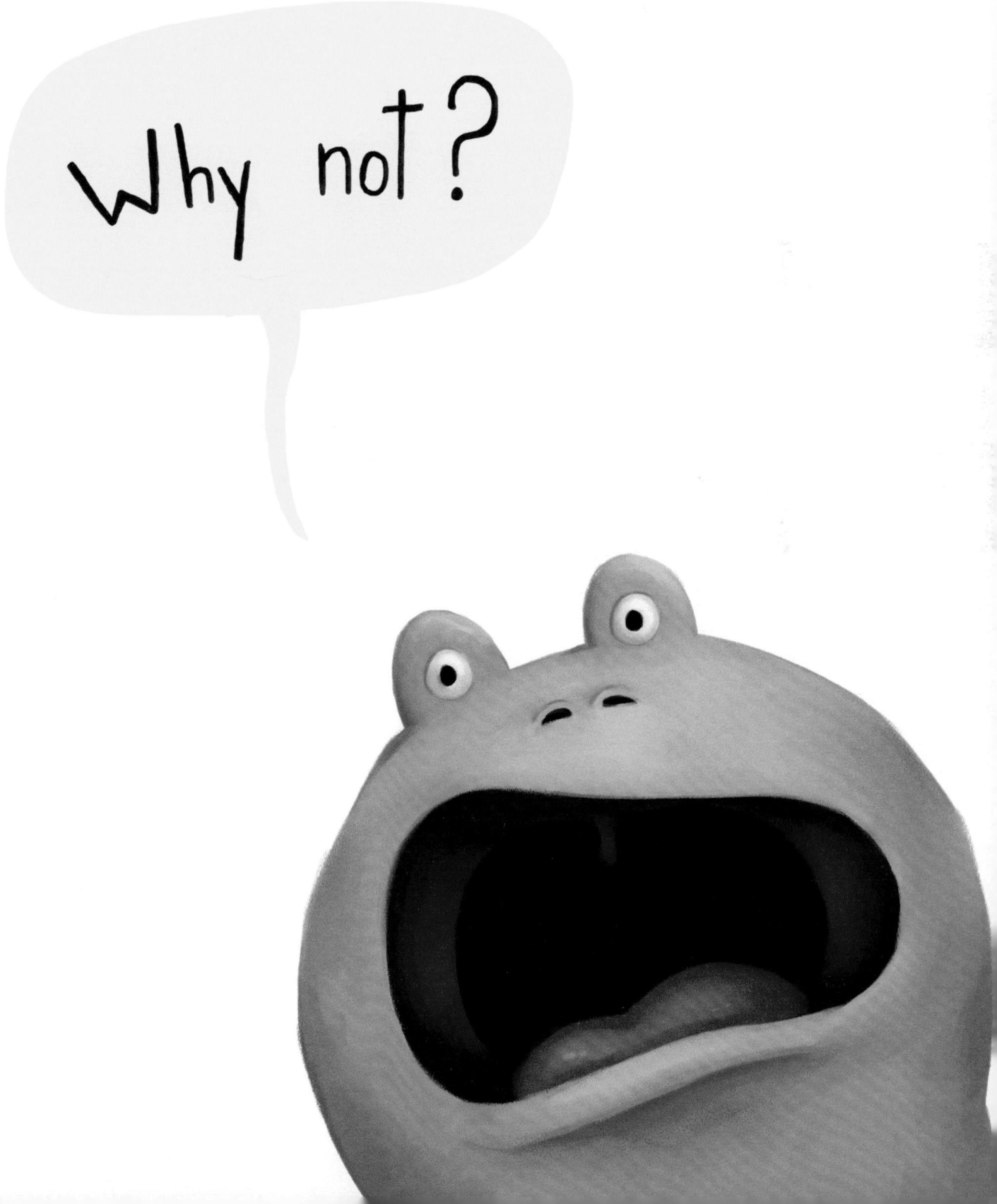
Why not?

You can't be a Pig.
Why not?
Most of all because you're a Frog. But also because you don't have a curly tail or eat garbage.
I can eat garbage.
Everyone says that until they eat garbage. Sorry, you can't be a Pig.

Of course you want to be an Owl! Being an Owl is the greatest thing ever.
Boy, would you love being an Owl.
So can I be an Owl, then?

No, of course not!
Why not?
1. You don't have wings.
2. You don't look wise.
3. You can't turn your head all the way around.
4. YOU ARE A FROG.

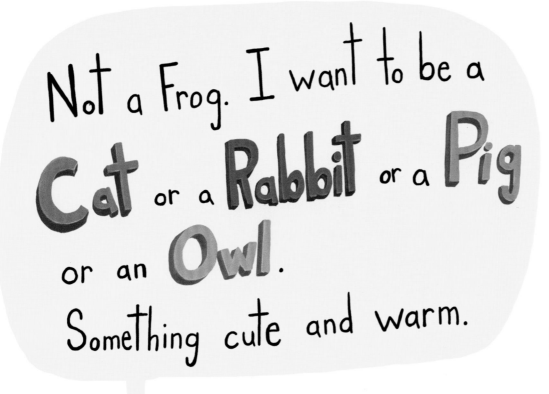

Not a Frog. I want to be a **Cat** or a **Rabbit** or a **Pig** or an **Owl**. Something cute and warm.

I'm going to let you in on a little secret....

And you are a Wet, Slimy, Bug-Eating, very lucky Frog.
You should just be happy you're not a Fly.

Dev Petty is one lucky customer. She used to work in the movies, and now she gets to write picture books, including *I Don't Want to Be a Frog* and *I Don't Want to Be Big*. Her hobbies include living in California, combining random words, and sandwich making. She lives in the San Francisco Bay Area with her husband, daughters, dogs, and a very mean cat.

Mike Boldt is an author and illustrator living in the countryside of Alberta, Canada. He is the illustrator of many children's books, including *I Don't Want to Be a Frog* and *I Don't Want to Be Big*. When he's not drawing, he's building snow forts and Lego spaceships with his three kids, or sharing laughs and his ice cream with his wife. He is very glad he's not a frog.